button moon

Button Moon:
The Ice Cream Van

Story and original designs by Ian Allen

Adapted from the Thames Television series
featuring the Playboard Puppet Theatre

Puppets and Settings by John Thirtle
and Rob Matson

A Thames Magnet Book

Daddy Egbert is very pleased because today he starts a new job. It's at the Tooti-Frooti Ice Cream Factory where Vanilla works. She had to start very early this morning.

Mr Spoon asks Daddy Egbert what sort of work it is. He is going to be driving the Ice Cream Van.

Daddy Egbert is a bit nervous. He's never driven an ice cream van on his own. Egbert asks if he can have a ride. No, it's not allowed. But while Daddy Egbert is out selling ice cream, Mr Tub, the owner of the factory, will show them round.

There's Vanilla. She works very hard filling ice cream tubs with vanilla ice cream. That is why her nickname is Vanilla. When the ice cream tubs are full they go over to Cherry. Her Syrup Rippling Machine pours ripples of cherry-flavoured topping on to the ice cream.

Hazel's machine crunches the nuts. They drop on to the ice cream before the lids are put on. Tina and Egbert think it must be very nice to work here. Everybody must eat lots and lots of ice cream. Mr Tub says they would soon get tired of it if they ate it every day.

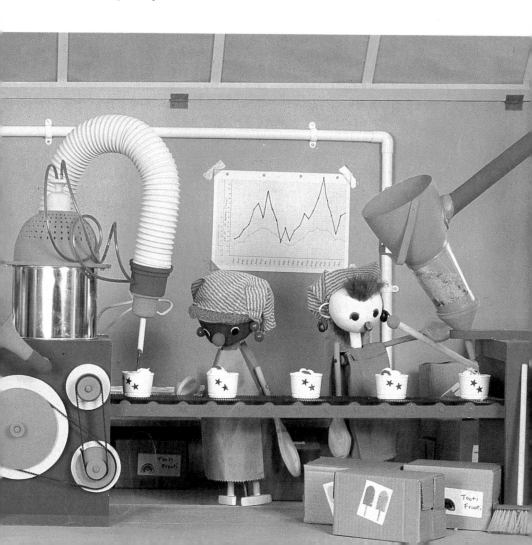

Mr Spoon thinks they ought to let them carry on with their work. Mr Tub has brought ice lollies for Tina and Egbert. They say thank you. Tina thinks they look a bit like the spaceship. Mr Spoon says it's time to leave for Button Moon.
5. . . 4. . . 3. . . 2. . . 1. . . Blast off!

The spaceship climbs up into Blanket Sky. Tina and Egbert can see the Ice Cream Factory below them.

Tina hopes that the next time they visit the factory they can find out how the ice lollies are made. Egbert can see they are getting closer to Button Moon. Mr Spoon presses the round button to make the spaceship land.

The spaceship lands on Button Moon. Freddy
Teddy is there to greet them. 'Hello everybody. I've
just bought a new door-bell for Rag Doll. It's in
this carrier bag.' DING-A-LING-A-LING.

'What's that noise?' asks Rag Doll.

'It's a brand new doorbell for you,' says Freddy Teddy. 'You never hear me calling when you're in the toy box. It's got a really loud ring. Listen.'

DING-A-LING-A-LING!

Rag Doll laughs, 'Everyone on Button Moon will be able to hear it. It's frightened the clockwork mouse.'

Freddy Teddy says, 'I'll fix it to the toy box straight away.'

'Not now,' replies Rag Doll. '*I'm* off to the Safari Park – why don't you come with me in the dumper truck?'

'That sounds a good idea,' says Freddy Teddy.
Rag Doll says, 'Don't forget your carrier bag.'

They drive off in the dumper truck. Rag Doll says, 'Freddy Teddy, in the Safari Park you have to stay in your car otherwise the big lions will get you.'

Freddy Teddy says, 'But we're not in a car – we're in a dumper truck. It's all open. That lion over there with the big teeth will be able to get us!'

'I'm not scared,' says Rag Doll. 'Can I hold your paw?'

She jumps beside Freddy Teddy and lands on the carrier bag. DING-A-LING-A-LING!

'The doorbell has frightened the lion. He's falling to pieces!' Freddy Teddy says, 'Just as well he was only painted on building bricks. I do like the elephant . . .'

'. . . and I like the painted pelican,' says Rag Doll.

'I like playing the Safari Park game,' says Rag Doll. 'Let's put the lion back together again.' Mr Spoon has brought the telescope from the spaceship. They all look through it to see what they can see.

Through the telescope they can see Brew the
Witch and Thunder the Dragon. They are off to get
some fish and chips for tea. Lightning the Cat is in
the garden, waiting for them to return with the
fish and chips.

Brew looks up and down the High Street for somewhere to park Thunder. He's too big to take into the fish and chip shop. Brew is lucky today – there is a vacant parking space right outside George's Fish and Chip Shop. 'Oh! Goody, goody!' Thunder can stay there while Brew goes inside for the cod and chips. 'Yummy, Yummy!'

Oh dear, Thunder can see someone coming. It is a traffic warden walking towards him. Brew has forgotten to put any money in the parking meter. She had better hurry up or Thunder will get a parking ticket!

Brew is too late. The traffic warden has seen Thunder. Well, he is the size of a double decker bus! She wonders where to put the parking ticket. Thunder doesn't have any windscreen wipers so she sticks the ticket to the end of Thunder's nose and marches off.

Thunder roars. Brew pops her head round the door to see if he is all right. Aaagh! She screams! She can see that Thunder has a parking ticket. She jumps up and down in a temper. If only she had her book of spells with her, she could have made the traffic warden disappear! And now Brew has lost her place in the queue – she'll never get her fish and chips!

Aaaatchoo! Thunder sneezes and blows the parking ticket away. Haha! He finds that very funny. At long last Brew has got her fish and chips. 'Tasty! Tasty!'

They hurry home and Brew unwraps them. She puts the fish on her plate and the steaming chips on Thunder's plate. Meeow! Lightning the Cat takes Brew's fish and whizzes out through the cat-flap as quick as lightning!

Never mind, Brew. Thunder will share his chips with you. Brew says, 'Thank you.' Then she sees the chips. 'Ugh!' Thunder has put such a lot of sauce on his chips. He likes tomato sauce, brown sauce, apple sauce and curry sauce! Yuk!

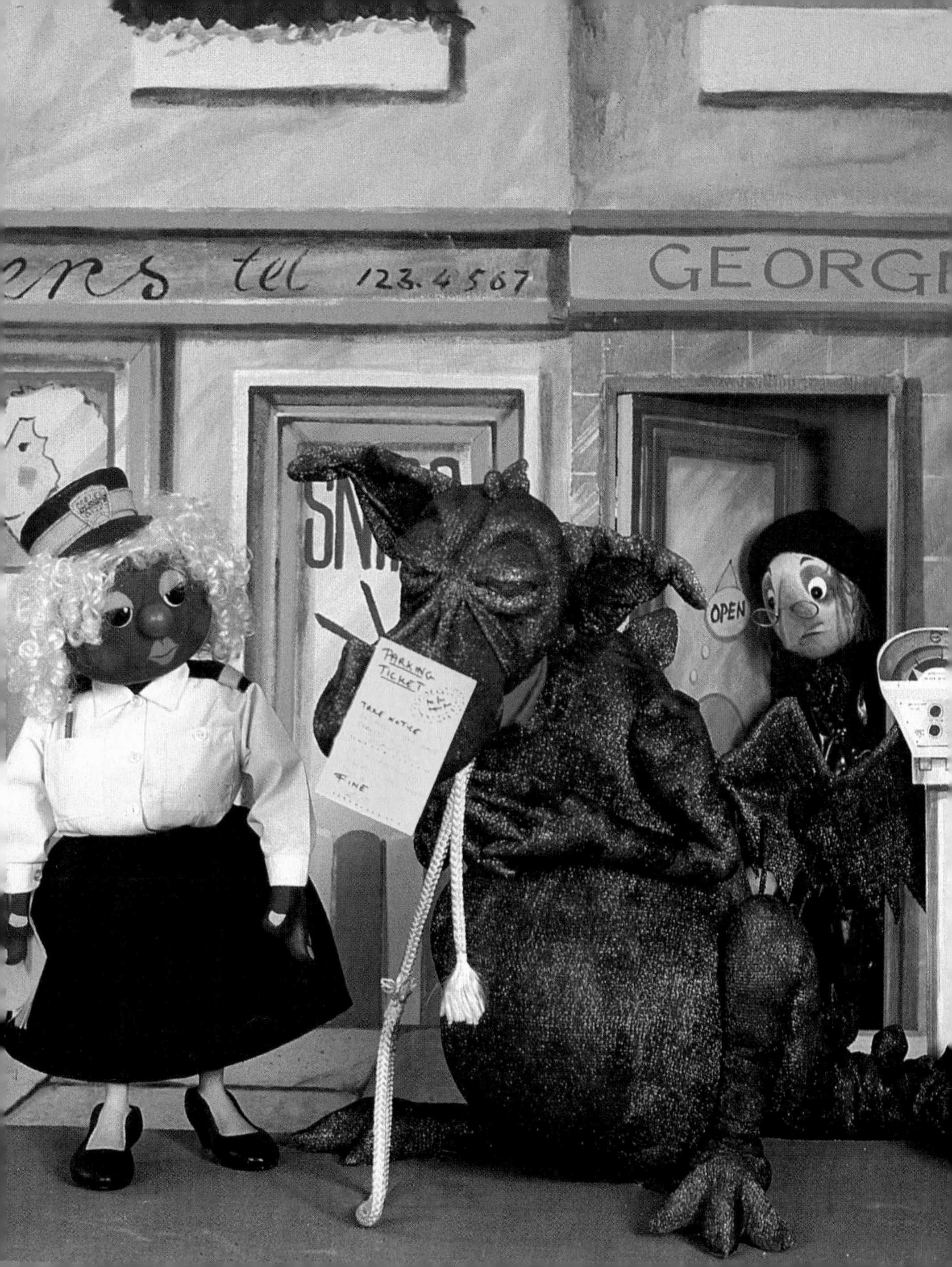
ers tel 123.4567
GEORG
OPEN
PARKING TICKET
TAKE NOTICE
FINE

Egbert asks if they can look through the telescope to find his Dad. That's a good idea! They see that Daddy Egbert is in trouble. There is smoke coming from the ice cream van! And it's Daddy Egbert's first day at work too! Tina asks if they can help.

Mr Spoon says they'll have to sell the ice creams for Daddy Egbert. Rag Doll has an idea. 'You can borrow my doorbell. Everyone will hear the Ding-a-ling-a-ling and come and buy the ice creams.' Mr Spoon thanks her. They climb into the spaceship. 5. . . 4. . .3. . . 2. . . 1. . . Blast off!

The spaceship is flying to the rescue. Egbert hopes the ice cream isn't melting. Mr Spoon presses the round button and the spaceship lands next to Daddy Egbert's ice cream van.

They are just in time. They help to load all the ice cream and the cornets and the wafers into the spaceship. Daddy Egbert puts a sign on the van to tell everyone it's broken down. Then they take off again to sell the ice creams.

The spaceship lands beside the block of flats where
Egbert lives. DING-A-LING-A-LING! The neighbours
hear the ringing sound coming from the spaceship.
They line up and buy the ice creams. Even Mrs
Spoon buys a choc ice! Daddy Egbert thanks them
all for helping.

This Magnet edition first published in Great Britain 1986 by
Methuen Children's Books Ltd, 11 New Fetter Lane, London EC4P 4EE
in association with Thames Television International Ltd
149 Tottenham Court Road, London W1P 9LL
Text © 1986 by Playboard Puppets
Photographs by Cressida Pemberton Pigott, © Thames Television International
Book design by Sue Ryall
Button Moon: The Ice Cream Van 0 423 01880 9
Printed in Great Britain